THE ADVENTURES OF HORACE HORRISE
BOOK 7

HORACE
HORRISE
CATCHES
A
SHOPLIFTER

John Hemming-Clark

© Searchline Publishing 2018
First edition 2018
ISBN: 978 1 897864 43 2
British Library Cataloguing in Publication Data available
Published by Searchline Publishing, Searchline House
Holbrook Lane, Chislehurst, Kent, BR7 6PE, UK

Tel: +44 (0)20 8468 7945
www.inyougo.webeden.co.uk

Printed in England by www.catfordprint.co.uk

OTHER BOOKS IN THE SERIES OF
THE ADVENTURES OF HORACE HORRISE

Dedicated to D S
Who's read most of my books -
but paid for none of them

"Of course I don't want to go to a cocktail party... If I wanted to stand around with a load of people I don't know eating bits of cold toast I can get caught shoplifting and go to Holloway." Victoria Wood

Horace Horrise catches a Shoplifter

Ravens patrol had just had what Horace would call a "fantastic evening." This was usually code for food having been consumed. Today was no exception. The scouts had finished their weekly troop meeting and Ravens were on their way home munching raspberry and Marmite pizza.

Scout Leader John, known to the scouts as "Skip," had introduced the evening as a "pizza oven" event and immediately the mention of a food word had the scouts' attention. "I've brought along four empty crisp boxes, one for each patrol. The other materials that your patrols will have at their disposal include a roll of silver foil, four metal coat hangers and some Sellotape. I'll also give you a pair of scissors and a thermometer. The crisp box is the basis of your oven...Yes Emily?"

Emily had already put her hand up in the air and was waving it frantically around as if trying randomly to swat a fly. For some reason, known only to children, it was impossible for adults to advance past the first in a series of instructions before one child would need some clarification even though, if they waited, the answer would invariably come further down the line and without any prompting. However, it did not matter how often this was explained, it was inevitable that the next time instructions were given, the scene would play itself out once more. John stopped talking and addressed Emily, raising an eyebrow.

"Please Skip, my mum has just spent thousands of pounds on a new oven and she's had it specially sprayed to match her kitchen and you think we're going to make something out of a few bits of tat that does the same only not as good and probably won't work? Why Skip? Why are we doing this when we can use a proper oven?" Skip looked at Emily, smiled and decided to explain.

"The answer, Emily, is simple. Your mother may have a Lacanche Classic Range Macon Cooker capable of prodigious output when needed but we can hardly take it on camp, can we? On the other hand you will always have what we're using on camp, especially crisp boxes, and empty ones at that." John returned to his monologue.

"Now then, all you have to do is reconfigure the lid to make a door by sticking the two or four flaps together, cover the box with three layers of silver foil making sure that you don't use Sellotape on the inside of the box, straighten out the coat hangers and poke through the sides to make a rack, then make a dish for the bottom of the oven to put the charcoal coals on that I will give you once you're ready for them. See what temperature the pizzas need to cook at, then, taking your ovens outside, put a few coals in that I have started on the campfire, on the tray at the bottom. Leave the oven for five minutes then check how hot it is. When the temperature is about right, after you've added or subtracted some coals, put the pizza on the rack, close the lid and wait ten minutes. After that lift the lid carefully and check that your pizza's piping hot. If it is you can eat it. Off you go!"

As an added incentive John told the scouts that if they worked quickly they would have time for two pizzas per patrol. This was music to Ravens' ears as it meant the difference between still hungry and not so hungry. Melanie announced, "Hurry and we can have one third of a pizza instead of one sixth!" Edward was unimpressed.

"I don't like any old flavour pizzas. I wonder what flavours

Skip has in mind to give us?"

"Don't be stupid, Edward," said Archie, frustrated by his friend's ability to look a gift horse in the mouth. "It doesn't matter what it says on the box, all pizzas are the same. They're dough and cheese and tomato and a few lumps of something. They have more or less the same ingredients and also taste the same as well. I bet if I gave you a margherita and told you it was a romana you would think that you had a romana."

"No I wouldn't, I would know exactly what it was. I would be able to tell after the first mouthful what it was," said Edward with conviction.

"Then we'll blindfold you when it's pizza tasting time and you can guess what it is," Archie challenged.

"Okay. And if I guess it right I'll get the whole pizza as long as I like it?" suggested Edward hopefully.

"Okay," Archie agreed.

The added incentive of a second pizza worked wonders for the scouts' productivity. With the oven linings being constructed at full tilt, Archie wandered up to John and casually asked him, "Sorry to sound a bit cautious Skip, but do you actually have enough pizzas for two per patrol?" Archie was not going to put himself out more than he had to only to find that John had only bought a couple of extras. He had good reason to be a little cautious for, if he were Skip, he would surmise that, on balance, there would be at least one, and most likely two or more, patrols that would be too slow to have time to get one pizza in their oven, let alone two - and cooked. But for once John had excelled

5

himself, helped by the special offer at his local supermarket.

"Yes, of course. In fact I've come more than prepared. I actually have twelve so that once you've all gone home Patrick and I and the young leaders can have one each."

"That's not fair," said Mel who had been listening in. "You've paid for them with scout money and it should be spent on scouts not leaders..."

"We are all scouts equally together," said John irritably. "It's just that some of us are leaders and some of us are being led..."

"Well if you read George Orwell's 'Animal Farm,'" Mel spat out, "you would know that some are more equal than others."

Archie wasn't going to stop Mel having her say, especially as he felt that she, for once, had a valid point, but at that particular moment he was more interested in testing Edward's assertion than following the argument concerning the literary justification of Skip scoffing an extra pizza. "The thing is, Skip, Edward reckons that he can tell the flavour of any pizza blindfolded so we wondered if we could at some point swap them over to really test him just in case he's thinking of cheating?"

"You can go better than that, Archie," John assured him, showing willing to be involved in the challenge. "Pizza toppings on chilled factory produced pizzas, which is what we have, can actually be peeled off the pizza in one, a bit like peeling a banana. As they normally have loads of gunk and cheese to hold the topping together, which is then plopped onto each pizza base as it goes along the conveyor

6

belt, it also peels off very easily. What I'll do is take the topping off one pizza and give you the base; you can then go and add what you think fit from the kitchen store cupboard." Archie did not need telling twice.

"Can I go now please, Skip?" Of course he could. Although scout leaders are meant to be made of sterner stuff - leading including encouraging, correcting including occasionally reprimanding - they are humans too and it was obvious by what Archie then did without be told not to, that John was as keen to find out how acute Edward's taste buds were as anybody else. However, John was certainly not fully ready for what Archie was going to put on the pizza by way of a new topping, he was thinking along the lines of essentially a topping swap, but Archie was keen to ensure that Edward had a much harder challenge. Out of Edward's sight John helped Archie to peel off a complete margherita topping which John then put on one of the other leaders' pizzas to make a double. Archie took the bare pizza base into the kitchen and had a hunt around the fridge in which was kept mostly leftover items from camp that were usually very out of date. First Archie added a layer of raspberry jam that had some grey fur on top of it. He then smeared spoonfuls of peanut butter, followed by a banana that was so black that when Archie peeled it it collapsed onto the pizza in a big dollop. Then he found some gherkins which he chopped up, a few smears of Marmite and a lemon curd yoghurt that smelt very off but which Archie decided wouldn't smell once it had been in the oven. "Waste not, want not," said Archie as he added the finishing touches.

Hawks were the first patrol to finish their oven. They had cut off the four flaps that made up the box lid, taped them together to make a door and then wrapped several layers of tin foil around the result. They had then expertly lined the

7

outside of the box and had taped the now door back onto the now oven and hinged it at the top so that it fell shut over the oven when required. John didn't like to tell them that foil on the exterior wasn't needed but felt that he could wait until the end of the evening and then mention it as part of a debriefing. Using a pair of tongs he passed Hawks a few coals which they poured into a silver foil dish on the oven floor. It was all going far too well, John thought. After all, in his experience, activities that involved fire normally had an unintended consequence or two. However he had thought too soon. After waiting five minutes for the oven to warm up it didn't let off a warm glow to indicate that it was ready to receive a pizza; it started to smoke. "Blimey," said Horace, not concentrating on what he was supposed to be doing, which would have been a far more useful exercise, "Hawks' oven is smoking like it's about to blow up and destroy the scout hut and there's not even a pizza in it yet!"

Hawks' Patrol Leader, Jack, saw what was happening and made a decision, that was probably not the most intelligent in the circumstances, to open the oven door in order that he might investigate what was going on inside. The rush of oxygen that was sucked in lifted the fire from smoking to flaming as the cardboard box suddenly burst into a furnace of orange fire. As it lay burning on the ground, black and charred, John lifted the door with a stick. Although it was more or less completely burnt out the thick charred cardboard had kept its shape as the door crumbled on being opened and John asked, peering at the inside and expecting to find some foil remnants, "Where's the lining?"

"On the outside," said Jack, sounding as if he were addressing a simpleton.

"That's fine, I don't mind that," said John agreeably, "but I told you to cover the box. Why would I mean the outside and certainly not just the outside? We're making an oven not a hob top." Then John's best-left-unsaid thoughts got the better of him. "If you had just one ounce of intelligence you would realise that you cook INSIDE an oven and if it isn't lined with something metallic then it's going to melt or burn."

Jack considered John's words but did not have time to answer as Emily was already wandering over, hands in pockets.

"That one won't be much good on camp will it, eh, Skip? And that sort of thing wouldn't have happened to my mum's cooker."

"Thank you for your input, Emily," said John shortly, "but would you might going and helping your own patrol?"

Emily shuffled back to Ravens leaving Hawks to extinguish the smoking ash. She found Ravens busy discussing the pizza situation. "Hawks' loss is our gain! We now have three extra pizzas between three teams. That means, er..." said Archie.

"One more per patrol," said Emily decisively.

"Gosh," said Archie, accepting her at her word. "If we slow down our oven-making so that we're last to finish then we might see the other two ovens burn down and then we would have one and um..."

"All of them," said Emily.

Unfortunately for Ravens, the other patrols were far more

successful with their linings, (after all they couldn't have been much worse, thought Horace), and soon it was time for the three remaining to start cooking. Skip advised the scouts that with two sets of racks, two pizzas could fit into each oven at once. Ravens were to cook one normal pizza and one "Guess the pizza topping" pizza for the competition (with one entrant). Skip blindfolded Edward with several scarves and one margherita and the dubious concoction were both placed in Ravens' oven. Almost straightaway a very sweet and sickly smell came wafting out of the box. Edward began to sniff like an excited dog that had just caught the scent of something very, very interesting and worthy of immediate investigation. There were familiar smells floating around but some very unusual ones also. After all, it wasn't every day that one would bake gone-off lemon curd yoghurt on its own let alone with a load of other unsuitable ingredients. After ten minutes Archie donned an oven glove and gingerly lifted the lid of Ravens' oven and peered inside, pronouncing their pizzas, "Done!" Carefully he extracted both from the oven with the other patrols watching on, some smiling, others grimacing. Archie put the pizzas on a plate each and cut started to cut them up into wedges.

"Come on then, Edward, try this one," goaded Archie. Mel led Edward over to the plate with the steaming concoction on it. Archie picked up a slice and placed it in Edward's outstretched hand. First Edward sniffed it, gingerly he licked it and finally he slowly bit into it. He chewed, stopped chewing, frowned, started chewing again and finally put the remains of the slice back down on the plate.

"It's like nothing I've ever experienced before," he said, putting on a serious face. "It's not too bad at all but if I was to hazard a guess I'ld say that that is what one would call,

10

um..."

The scouts could not wait for Edward to give his answer. For they felt that he was undoubtedly seconds away from walking into a very large trap. Was he going to say "margherita," maybe "romana," possibly "Hawaiian?" Whatever he said they were all going to laugh uncontrollably and congratulate Archie on his fantastic coup. Edward: Nil. Rest of Scouts: One. They were all to be disappointed.

"I think," Edward said finally, "I think that is what you would call a 'scout pizza.'"

"Well, you're not wrong there," said John who had been watching and listening as carefully and as intently as the scouts. "I'm going to give you full marks for that." Edward said nothing, he just smiled to himself.

"Would you like any more of it?" Archie asked hopefully. If he was going to lose the competition, the next best outcome would be that at least he could make Edward sick.

"No thanks, Archie." The truth was that Edward felt that whatever the concoction was, and he was relieved that no one had forced him to name the pizza - not that that was in any way possible - and that all had been satisfied with his not giving a wrong answer, if he actually knew what was in it he might have suddenly felt rather ill. The other Ravens weren't so reticent and once the margherita had been eaten, John gave them a slice of concoction to take home, not that it lasted that long and was mostly completely finished soon after they had passed through the scout hut gates. It may have had a selection of unusual ingredients on it, but the baked mixture of sweet and savoury was perfectly palatable.

Ravens all felt that "scout pizza" was a great name for any pizza with an unusual and esoteric topping.

At flag down John reminded the scouts of the following day's activity. They had been told several times already over the past few weeks but John was of the firm opinion that every time he repeated something one more scout would remember. This meant that, for maximum response, everything would have to be mentioned around thirty times - and double that for the parents. "We're going down to the supermarket in the high street for a spot of bag packing. We're raising funds that will benefit all of you. We would like to purchase a new patrol tent. The one we're after sleeps ten, you can stand up in it and it has a built in groundsheet." The scouts thought that this was an excellent idea and so all nodded in agreement.

"If there's any money left over we can go and have a round or two of adventure golf at Swingers." The scouts nodded in agreement again and a rumble of happy chatter momentarily filled the air. Swingers was a favourite of Ravens with its two crazy golf courses, Grunt and Groan, side by side, to test even the most proficient of putters. Although it had been some time ago, memories were still very fresh when it came to Emily putting a hole in one on the seventeenth hole of the Grunt course. Built like a mini volcano with the crater as the hole, the only way to approach it, Horace maintained, was to shoot to the bottom of the volcano, then make a swift, decisive and accurate putt up the side. Emily, however, had come along and shattered all illusions as to the hole's complexity. She made a swift, decisive and accurate putt from the tee-off and scored a hole-in-one. Ravens applauded. Emily beamed. Horace scowled. Ever since then he had avoided Grunt, choosing instead the slightly easier Groan course. Even when they had the opportunity to do both courses, one after the other, Horace had chosen to do the Groan course twice. He had never been allowed to forget it.

"Make sure that you're there," John encouraged. "Ten a.m. prompt; ready for a few hours' action. And don't forget your scout shirts and scarves. Cleaned and ironed. And as a special incentive, the pair that raises the most can get to keep the difference between what they raise and the second highest pair."

The scouts' eyes sparkled. This could be the opportunity to raise a huge amount of cash. "Miss Humbug - here we come with enough money to keep us in sweets for the rest of the year!" thought more than one scout.

"I suppose your mother will be helping you out by doing her shopping tomorrow?" suggested Mel to Horace after the scouts had been dismissed. "Unlike my mother who would never be seen dead in *that* supermarket."

"Hardly," said Horace. "My mummy never goes there either. In fact I don't think much of Chislehurst goes there. Probably just the people from Mottingham from what I can gather."

"So how would you know that," asked Mel, "if you never go there?"

"Actually, *I* do go there," emphasised Horace. "It's just that when I do I'm doing it for mummy 'cos she wouldn't want to be seen dead in there either. I think that she would probably rather starve than have to shop in that store."

***

"So what exactly does 'bag packing' involve Archie?" Horace asked as they left the scout hut and wandered into the woods for a quick game of tag before finally heading home. "I thought the only time someone did bag packing was when they were leaving home."

"It's quite simple Horace," Archie explained patiently. "It's something we have to do now and then. It's where you stand by the check-out all day filling shoppers' bags with their groceries."

"That sounds really dull," said Horace feeling more than a little horrified at the thought of having to spend a few precious minutes, let alone most of his Saturday in a supermarket. He felt that a far easier option, if Skip was in need of some extra funds, was simply to ask the parents. The element of community cohesion and making the scouts more visible to the local residents was completely overlooked by Horace. As was the fact that a proportion of money raised was always given to another charity. "Don't you get bored?" he asked, wondering whether he would need to wake up in the morning with a sudden phantom illness.

"No, not really," said Archie, much to Horace's relief. "But you need to bring a pack of chewing gum with you. Firstly, we get paid 'cos the shoppers put money in a collecting tin and the money gets used to buy some decent kit or a day out or sweets or something scouty related. Secondly, we can also collect the supermarket's 'Vitality Vouchers' that they give to the shoppers and it's one for every ten pounds spent; these we can use to exchange for kit at the end of the year. For every five thousand we get we can get a posh tent, one of the fun three or four-man ones. Thirdly, we work in pairs so there's always someone to talk to when it's quiet and fourthly, when we ask if someone would like to have their bags packed and they say, 'No', which isn't very many of them, then I make sure that I drop a piece of chewed chewing gum in their bags so that everything inside sticks together. Fifthly, although most people watch you like a hawk, if they're not taking any notice and they look like someone who's not going to give you any money, it's always fun to mix things up a bit and put something like a warm cooked chicken in with their ice cream. That way you can sometimes start a leak before they've even got to their car. Last year Melanie put a plastic squeezy thing of maple syrup, which is really expensive, in a bag first - on its side - then dropped, and I mean dropped, a two kilo bag of sugar and a one-and-a-half kilo bag of flour on top. Both bags split and she said she heard the maple syrup bottle 'pop' but the woman whose shopping it was was too busy talking to her friend on her 'phone to notice. When Melanie looked in the bag it was all starting to congeal together in a huge sticky mess like an enormous cake mixture that had gone wrong so she quickly put the woman's newspaper on top to cover it all up and then continued as if nothing had happened. And then the worse bit was she got a huge donation and some Vitality Vouchers and the woman said, 'Thank you Melanie,' even though Melanie didn't know who she was but the woman obviously did. So, yes, the best thing to do to liven things up is make sure that you put the squidgy things in first like berries and yoghurts and cakes and eggs and then everything else on top but best to do it to people who you don't know and if you're unsure then say, 'Hello, have you come far?' Then at least you have a chance of avoiding doing something nasty to someone your parents may know or you may bump into in the street at a later date. The other thing is that often shoppers will talk to you and ask you questions. You can have a really great competition with your pair to see who can tell the most lies. It's one point for a lie and two points for a real whopper that no one challenges. So if someone asks you how long you've been a scout, if you tell them that actually you're a beaver still, it's just that you're quite small and then look sad and if they don't seem suspicious then that's two points. If they ask what we're collecting for say it's for our subs as our parents can't afford them so we have to do this, then look sad also. Then you get a point but you may also get loads more money. If you have someone old and on their own like an old man who's bent over and he's just come in for a pint of milk and he has really scruffy clothes on he could easily be a millionaire. So ask him if he wants his milk packed and when he says 'no' which he probably will do look sad. These things should get people to donate more 'cos they feel sorry for you."

"Well, I agree that that doesn't sound very boring," said Horace once Archie had finished his monologue. Horace felt that some of it sounded a little dubious and somewhat underhand but decided that as they were offering a service then they should be paid.

"It's not like begging," said Archie as he thought that Horace looked a little unsure. "We are actually doing something even if the shoppers didn't know that we would be doing it when they first came into the store."

The following day Horace, having decided not to be sick, told his mother that he was going bag packing to raise funds for a new tent.

"Good idea," said Karen Horrise. "A bit of community enterprise. And you get a new tent for an honest day's work."

Soon Horace found himself standing outside the supermarket with Charlie when John arrived. "Some parents have 'phoned their scouts in sick," he said. "I can't imagine why," he added sarcastically. "As for you two I've put you together on the first till. See how much you can raise! As a special incentive, the pair that raises the most can get to keep the difference between what they raise and the next highest pair," he reminded the enthusiastic couple.

"Game on!" thought Horace and Charlie to themselves.

Once the rest of the scouts with stronger stomachs had arrived, which included all Ravens, they walked quietly and solemnly into the supermarket to take up their positions. Horace and Charlie were given a collecting bucket each with their names on the bottom and told that they could start straightaway on Angela's till at the far end. There was no training, no advice. John always thought that even the most inept of scout bag packers would be met with sympathy. He felt that there was never anything that could go very wrong. But that was before Horace.

Angela was dressed in the rather banal supermarket uniform but her personality shone through her conversation, hair and makeup. She resembled someone very famous but Horace couldn't quite put his finger on who it was. She was probably much older than she looked but she smiled warmly as Horace and Charlie approached so probably wasn't all bad, Horace decided. As Horace and Charlie went closer she beckoned them over and asked them their names. "I'm Angela," she said. "Come and put your buckets down here." She patted the end of the till by the receipt printer. "We'll have some fun today! This is the busiest till and the day will fly by. Us cashiers normally

17

have an unofficial competition to see which till can raise the most and I love to win!" she purred. "I'll give you some pointers as we go along, but if you want to win also we will!"

"How can you help?" asked Horace cautiously.

"To start with I know many of the customers. They come to my till even though my queue may be longer. I'll tell them about the scouts and what you're collecting for. That sort of stuff. Butter them up a bit. What are you collecting for?" she asked curiously.

"Err, I'm not sure," said Charlie feeling a little dejected that he didn't have a ready answer to Angela's question.

"It that case," said Angela, totally nonplussed. "I'll tell them that you're raising money for the St Rochelle Hospice."

"Okay," said Charlie who felt that a little deceit was justified if they would be at least directing part of their fundraising in that direction. "Where is it?"

"'St Rochelle Hospice?'" Angela laughed. "It doesn't exist. I just made it up. I went to La Rochelle on holiday a few years ago. Sounds like a good enough name as any! No adult will ask 'Where is it?' because they will not want to show that they don't know. Don't worry about it boys!" she added when she saw that they both looked worried. "You can't be held criminally responsible at your age. We're in it to win it! When the old duffers come through I'll try and slide an extra tenner out of them. They mostly still pay cash. There are cameras everywhere but they don't record sound so if I look confident in what I'm doing then all is well. If the oldies have a tappy card I'll tell them that it hasn't gone through and they'll pay twice or I'll input an extra fiver and

18

put it down as a delivery charge or I'll give them a car parking ticket because you need one now to have free parking but I'll tell them that it costs a fiver now to park and I'll..."

"Just a second," said Horace. "Isn't this all a bit...?"

"Yes!" said Angela, also avoiding the 'dishonest' word. "But Chislehurst is a place that for too long has been the sanctuary of inherited wealth, the undeserving rich, the pompous plutocrats. Come the revolution when there's a complete realignment with the proletariat..." Angela suddenly stopped her tirade and turned her attention back to the present and her manager. "Quick, look busy, suit's coming."

Horace and Charlie looked over and saw a young man dressed in a smart dark grey suit and supermarket tie strolling over. Angela buried herself in her till and the conveyor belt starting to move. He nodded at the boys and gave a little cough. Angela looked up. Suit nodded in her direction and she smiled faintly, pressing a button down by her waist. A large "1" on top of a pole above her head lit up and a couple of shoppers wandered over with their baskets.

Mel and Emily had also wandered over behind the till and were watching Team Horace set up. "Hiya losers!" Emily shouted. "Girl power is going to win hands down today!"

Horace turned round and smiled at the pair of keen and excitable young girls. Horace wasn't sure how the girls won at most competitions but today they had more than met their match! By hook or by crook Horace and Charlie were going to win. And win big!

Horace started packing and Charlie started chatting. Initially Charlie was chatting to Horace and ignoring the shoppers but soon they realised that if they chatted to each other then not only would they not be able to ask the shoppers if they would like to have their bags packed, but also the shoppers wouldn't make a donation so they quickly decided to become a little more focussed. Meanwhile Angela was already working overtime, telling each shopper who asked for them that "Vitality Vouchers" were all being donated to the scouts that day. Most shoppers didn't argue and those that did were met with a, "Since when was your need greater than those of St Rochelle Hospice?" as she passed the vouchers to Horace or Charlie for them to put in their buckets. No one commented further.

After a few profitable minutes with the pair slowly gaining more confidence, Horace suddenly announced, nodding over Charlie's shoulder, "Oh, look. Look at this little old lady coming through. I can sense Angela rubbing her hands already. Let's butter her up as well and get a big donation. I bet she's a millionairess."

"Gosh, she's a bit overdressed isn't she?" said Charlie critically as he looked to the other end of the till and spied Horace's target for himself. "'Overdressed' as in loads of clothes not 'overdressed' as in posh clothes for the supermarket," was Horace's thought. Horace was completely correct in his belief that the little old lady was indeed little and old. It was also correct that she was also overdressed although "bit" was something of an understatement. Despite it being a fairly warm autumnal day the little old lady was wearing a thick beige woollen coat that almost reached down to her ankles and a matching hat that was so tall that it resembled, in shape if not material, a police officer's traditional helmet. It covered any hair that she might have still possessed as well as her ears and even her eyebrows. The little old lady stopped at the start of the till and placed a carton of milk, a bar of chocolate and a box of six eggs on the conveyor belt.

"C'mon," said Horace. "We can make some money here." The little old lady smiled sweetly at Angela as she passed alongside her and stopped next to Charlie who was unintentionally blocking her from moving any further. Angela said, "Hallo Lady Willit. It's lovely to see you. You're looking so well!" Angela turned and winked at Horace as she started to scan the items. Horace peered round Charlie and asked obsequiously, "I was just wondering if you would mind if we packed your groceries for you, madam. It would give us the greatest pleasure to..."

"No, thank you," she replied brusquely as she tried to bustle past.

"On, come on. It's free. It doesn't cost anything," said Horace who was rapidly gaining even more confidence (maybe too much) in speaking to the shoppers. Normally Horace would not have pursued the matter, but this particular customer was not at all like any of the other older folk that Horace and Charlie had so far met that morning. The oldies were usually more than happy to stop and chatter, so much so that the pair were often asked by Angela to get a move on as her queue was getting unacceptably long and the suit might appear at any moment to tell her to process units (which is what the supermarket referred to customers as) more quickly. Horace thought that he was not going to let Lady Willit go quite so lightly for, as a Lady, she was probably worth trying to "butter up" a little bit more, to get her onside, to wear her down, to encourage her into maybe making a large(r) donation.

"We're collecting for those who need our help – the poor, the dispossessed, those without homes." When Horace still didn't receive any response he added, "And St Rochelle Hospice." Still there was no reply so he continued, somewhat darkly, "You wouldn't want to have to face the creator's wrath having not helped those who needed it most and..."

"You could always donate your Vitality Vouchers if you like," added Charlie in an attempt further to pile on the pressure.

"Didn't spend enough," Lady Willit suddenly and unexpectedly murmured, all the while executing a passable impression of a tennis player making a backhand pass. "Now let me through," she muttered as she began to put her purchases in her small cotton shopping bag. She picked up the carton of eggs and waved it at Horace threateningly.

"'Now let me through' what?" Charlie asked without even thinking, so regularly did he hear it at home in the kitchen or at the dinner table that it had become embedded in his subconscious.

"Please, now," she hissed, pushing Horace aside with her elbow. She looked up and made eye contact for the first time. "Move!" she growled angrily, but Horace didn't. He stayed put. Rooted to the spot. Instinctively he knew that perhaps something wasn't right. In fact, he thought, something was most definitely very wrong. Why was she asking Horace to move? Why was she almost pleading? It sounded as if she were desperate, as if, at that particular moment, she wanted to be anywhere but in Horace's presence in the supermarket. She could not, however, go very far as she was trapped in the aisle between the two cashier stations with an advancing trolley behind and Horace in front. "I must..." but hardly had she started her sentence when something totally unexpected happened. Unexpected but not anything that was going to cause the two scouts much distress. She dropped the eggs back onto the packing area and grabbed the metal edge of the cashier station with both hands. "I...I..." The blood was rapidly draining from her face and her healthy glow turned to a bluish grey as she struggled to speak. The scouts knew what to do.

"Quick Horace," said Charlie. "Grab hold of her under her arms and lower her gently to the ground." Angela stood up and put her hand to her mouth as if about to scream. "It's okay Angela. It's not a problem," said Charlie, "we can sort this. We know what to do." Before Lady Willit had even been fully lowered to the ground a security guard - dressed in a dark blue suit with a badge pinned to his lapel that said, "FRANK: REVENUE PROTECTION," - had already appeared along with John in his capacity as a responsible leader, the other scouts in their capacity of mostly level one qualified first aiders, another member of staff carrying a large green folder with "Accident Report Forms" on the cover and who herself was also a first aider plus a number of other shoppers, one of whom cried out, "Oh my goodness, it's Lady Willit!" She was obviously known to a number of local shoppers, if not the scouts. Even a minor incident such as a faint seemed quickly to be gathering a disproportionate amount of attention from others in the supermarket.

"Is she breathing?" asked John concernedly.

"Yes," said Charlie who could hear Lady Willit gently

panting although her eyes were closed.

"Then she's probably just fainted," said John calmly, "so you know what to do. Let's try that first."

"Lift her legs up, Horace," commanded Charlie. "Let's direct the blood into her brain where it's needed and away from her legs where it's not for the time being." Horace lifted them up as directed.

"Good," said John who was keen to be seen to be in control of the situation with so many gathered round the confined space where Lady Willit had decided to be taken ill. "Now hold them there, Horace. Charlie, undo her coat; she's probably in danger of overheating." As Charlie started to undo the large buttons on Lady Willit's thick woollen coat she unexpectedly started to stir. John smiled to himself thinking that the scouts would have more confidence on their own next time such an event occurred.

"I must...leave me...off...go..." said Lady Willit. Her words came out slowly - stuttering and monosyllabic.

"Excuse me but I'm the first aider for this store," said a voice behind John. He turned and saw the young lady with the green folder staring at the patient. Without looking at John she said, "Please can you fill this in as your scouts are involved? It's an Accident Report Form."

"Yes, we will in a minute," said John, continuing to keep command of the situation. "The form can wait. The form's not going to help the patient. Let's just get her back on her feet first and given her age be ready to call for an ambulance." At the mention of the word "ambulance" Lady Willit opened her eyes and looked blankly up at the supermarket ceiling. Horace and Charlie followed her gaze and were surprised at what they noticed. They had never properly looked up before. They had just assumed that there would be ceiling. Instead they also found banks of lights of various types - florescent, LED and directional, wires, brackets, poles and loads of round black blobs the size of golf balls that Horace assumed were the cameras.

"It's okay," said Horace gently. "You've just fainted. But there are loads of people looking after you."

"When you're ready we'll stand you back up," said Charlie, "and you won't even have to make a donation."

"But you can if you want to," added Horace, keen not to let a good deed go unrewarded by the recipient.

"I'm ready now!" Lady Willit suddenly pronounced, coherently and assuredly, as if nothing had happened.

"Help me up now!" she commanded, waving her hands in the air as if trying to grab hold of something.

Horace and Charlie complied. They leant over and put one of their arms each under hers and lifted Lady Willit carefully to her feet.

"You'll be making a donation now I expect?" asked the ever-hopeful Horace, keen to make sure Lady Willit was aware of what was expected, by Horace at least.

"Stuff your donation you oily oik," she said abruptly, totally unexpectedly and completely out of character. "Where's me 'at?" she added, patting her head. Horace noted that her grey hair was soaking wet and concluded that she must have been sweating heavily. "Hardly surprising with a thick knitted hat," he thought.

"It's on the floor," said Horace making no move to pick it up as he didn't particularly want to let go of Lady Willit and watch her slump back down.

"Pick it up for Lady Willit and I'll hold onto her," instructed John, realising that the patient had still not completely regained the strength in her legs.

"I'll do it meself," she said quickly, attempting to reach down but with her hand hardly reaching beyond her knees.

"Here, let me," said Charlie who had already let go, not giving Lady Willit a chance to get to her hat first, but who was wondering why she kicked him as he bent down. "Cor, it's a bit heavy," said Charlie as he picked up the large woolly mass of headwear.

"Put it in me bag, now!" she demanded, looking around for her carrier.

"What have you got in there? Stolen goods?!" asked Horace confidently and with a smirk. Horace had learnt some time ago that if one said something with a smile one could say almost anything, a bit like a mediaeval jester taking advantage of his ostensibly lowly position to speak the uncomfortable truth to his employer the monarch. Horace took the hat from Charlie under the pretence of putting it in the shopping bag but looking inside instead. "Oh, look," he said putting his finger in the hat and touching something ice cold and clammy. "I've found a frozen chicken! I wonder how that got there?" Charlie put his hands into the hat and pulled out a large organic free-range Suffolk Black. "Well it

26

wouldn't have flown in there I don't expect," said Charlie. A collective gasp emanated from the small crowd.

"I think you'ld better come with me," said Frank, taking Lady Willit's arm firmly in one hand and her shopping bag, hat and chicken in the other, then leading Lady Willit back into the store and disappearing between the aisles to the safety, security and sanctuary of a small, anonymous office, the entrance of which was a thick metal number-coded door situated behind a freestanding display of tins of chocolates, followed by the lady with the folder shuffling on attentively behind.

"Looks like we've caught a thief," said Charlie to his companion.

"I thought thieves were all men," replied Horace innocently.

The pair continued their bag packing but more quietly - for a short while at least. Even Angela did not have so much to say and seemed more than a little subdued as the three of them individually went over in their minds the events that had so recently unfolded. However, any new customer would not have known anything untoward had just taken place. Those shoppers that had witnessed the drama had long since left the store with their purchases and everything was back to normal save Lady Willit waiting in Frank's office for a police car to come and take her away for questioning. Horace and Charlie had indeed caught a thief - a shoplifter - and both were firmly of the opinion, although they did not admit it to each other, that catching crooks was far more interesting than melting a shopper's ice cream or chilling their roast chicken. They did come close to lying a few times, but only inasmuch as they decided to swap names for a while but even this became too confusing.

When Horace called "Charlie," Charlie asked, "Are you calling yourself?" and they both giggled. It was probably only because they had caught a thief that they weren't ticked off by the suit who had been walking up and down the store behind the tills since the incident.

Angela was also soon back on form and was busy passing Vitality Vouchers to the boys, along with an occasional banknote or two in between customers, and plenty of loose change.

Horace considered their best customer could potentially be the man who would have passed in the street as Lady Willit's spouse. Elderly and dishevelled, he came slowly up to Angela's till and placed his basket on the conveyor belt with his few small items still in it. In his other hand he held a tatty but well-made dark brown leather wallet with some sort of crest on it. It was stuffed full of notes. "Good morning Mr Gibbs!" Angela greeted him. "And how are you today?" she asked obsequiously, keeping eye contact with mostly the top of his head as she removed the items from his basket and dropped it into the mysterious void beside her.

"I'm very well, today Angela," he replied, without looking up. "I'm having lunch with Lord Couper on Monday. I haven't seen him for quite a while and we need to catch up on the new reforms that the government is proposing regarding the Baker proposition."

Angela nodded sagely. She knew that Mr Gibbs was, or had been, an eminent QC but she hadn't the faintest idea what he was talking about and she wasn't afraid to tell him. "Oh, Mr Gibbs, that sounds so exciting! But I must say, I really don't know what any of it means other than the bit about you having lunch."

"'Your' having lunch, Angela."

"I am, yes, but not quite yet."

"No," replied Mr Gibbs patiently. "It's not 'you having lunch,' it's 'your.'" Angela smiled.

"I still don't know what you're talking about, but the important thing is that I have two bag packers helping me today. They're scouts. They're raising funds."

Mr Gibbs turned his attention away from Angela and faced Horace and Charlie - at least the top of his head did. "That's an excellent idea, promoting community and helping others. Which scout group are you from?" he enquired.

"If you lifted your head and looked at our arms you would see our name badges," thought Horace.

"3rd Chislehurst," they both replied earnestly. "Things are looking up even if Mr Gibbs isn't!" they both thought.

"'3rd Chislehurst!'" Mr Gibbs repeated. "What a coincidence! I was in 3rd Chislehurst when I was a young man. We used to have such fun running around in the great outdoors. I remember once when we made bows and arrows using strips of wood, doweling and string. They were extremely powerful. We put fins on the arrows and we had a competition to see who could fire theirs the furthest. I can't remember who won but what I do remember is we weren't allowed to have points on the arrows so the first thing Reg - he was my best friend - and I did the following day was whittle a point on all of our arrows. Then we went to the large field by the farm and set up a target on the oak tree. Reg got a direct hit first shot then it was my go. The bad news was I missed. The good news was I hit one of Farmer Fermor's pigs. It squealed, breathed its last and flopped over. We were flabbergasted. It's not that easy to kill a pig yet I had done it in one! However we could hardly leave it in the field and neither could we go and own up to Farmer Fermor as to what had happened." Mr Gibbs raised his head and finally looked at Horace and Charlie. "Can you guess what we did? We..."

Just at this crucial moment suit came over and stood by Angela's till. Angela leant over and said, "Tell us another time Mr Gibbs as I'm just about to get into trouble for not processing a sufficient amount of units." Suit stood as Angela scanned Mr Gibbs' items before reminding her that she was scheduled for a one o'clock break. He then wandered back down the line.

"Quick," said Horace, "tell us the rest of the story."

Mr Gibbs looked at Horace confusedly. "Tell you the rest of what story?"

"You know," said Horace, feeling more than a little frustrated. "About the pig that you and Reg shot."

Mr Gibbs breathed in and puffed out his chest. "I have never shot a pig in the whole of my life. And what are you two doing standing there?" he asked accusingly.

"We're bag packing," said Charlie, totally nonplussed by Mr Gibbs' behaviour. Adults of half the age of Mr Gibbs were capable of saying the daftest of things as well as forgetting what they were talking about so Mr Gibbs was completely absolved, even though he didn't realise that he was seeking any forgiveness in the first place. "And we've just packed your bag," Charlie added.

"You'll be wanting some money then?"

"Yes please," said Horace expectantly.

"What are you collecting for?"

"St Rochelle Hospice," said the pair. This bought a sudden and unexpected response from Mr Gibbs. He put one hand on the side of the checkout and said quietly, "That's where my darling wife Elizabeth spent her last days. We were out in Algeria when she was taken very ill. She was looked after so well." Mr Gibbs put down his shopping and his wallet and put his hand to his head, still clutching the checkout with the other, as a tear ran down his crumpled cheek.

"But why 'St Rochelle Hospice?'" he asked. Angela looked worried. Charlie looked at Angela then announced that he needed to go to the toilet and rushed off.

"'Cos my grandma lived in Algeria also," said Horace suddenly, "and she spent her last days in the hospice and the scouts thought that it was as good enough a place as any to send our fundraising money."

"Excellent," said Mr Gibbs as he picked up his wallet and paid for his shopping (in cash) then put two fifty pound notes, one each, in the two boys' buckets. "Maybe they had met. How long ago was this?"

"Last Wednesday," said Horace, who buy now was on auto-pilot, not even thinking about what was coming out from

31

his mouth.

"Strange," said Mr Gibbs as he put down his wallet again, picked up his shopping and looked around as if scanning the packing area before shuffling past, his head reinstating its downwards droop, "I didn't think that it was still around, whatever it was we were talking about."

"One hundred pounds!" hissed Horace to Angela as Mr Gibbs made his way out of the store. "I think we can win this!"

"And he's left his wallet behind!" said Angela, picking it up from the packing area and waving it at Horace. Horace grimaced.

"Don't worry, Horace," said Angela. "I'm not a thief. In any case I'm on camera."

"How did he manage to leave his wallet behind?" asked Horace with a frown. "He had it in his hand."

"He put it down to pick up his shopping and I put a load of Vitality Vouchers on top of it. Don't worry, he'll soon be back. And here he comes now," said Angela looking over Horace's shoulder.

"Forgotten something, Mr Gibbs?" said Angela smiling.

"I seem to have mislaid my wallet," he replied, looking confused and sounding very upset. "It has my bus pass in it."

"Here it is," said Angela cheerfully, handing it over. "Horace here found it. You left it on the counter when you were

32

righting yourself after talking about St Rochelle Hospice."

"Were we?" asked Mr Gibbs. He took his wallet and before stuffing it back inside his jacket he opened it and gave Horace another fifty pound note. "Finders' fee," he said as he turned and walked out once more.

Angela continued serving and soon Charlie had returned. "How d'you get out of that one Horace?" he asked as they continued their packing.

"Thank my grandma," said Horace, not fully answering Charlie's question. "Who's now died in Algeria instead of Wilmington. The fact of the matter is, we're now one hundred and fifty pounds up after Mr Gibbs' visit."

"Let's hope he comes back after lunch," Charlie sniggered, "and we can do it all over again; the forgetful old duffer."

As one o'clock drew ever closer Horace and Charlie became ever speedier. They were to be allowed a half hour break, subconsciously reckoning that if they worked quicker then the break would come sooner. They were just about to slouch off to the staff restroom when Angela turned and hissed, "Boys, look lively! It's Dr Godfrey!" The boys looked up the line of waiting customers and quickly decided that Dr Godfrey was second. He was smart casually dressed in a sports jacket, thick cotton checked open-necked shirt, dark corduroy jeans and tan brogues. He was patiently waiting behind a distressed and exhausted-looking young couple, the female appearing very pregnant, with one of the larger size trolleys, but there was not much in it apart from a baby. Rather than put the youngster in the baby seat frame with its legs dangling into the trolley it had actually been placed in the trolley and was rattling around with the groceries -

until the items for purchase were picked up and plopped on the conveyor belt by the red-eyed frazzled father along with the baby. The couple pushed the trolley past Angela and waited. The baby advanced towards her and came to a stop by the weighing platform in front of the scanner. She picked up the baby and said to the couple, who still hadn't noticed what they had done, and said, "It won't scan."

"Just put it back on the shelf then," said the father absentmindedly, "we need to get Albert fed," before his wife realised what had happened, gasped almost inaudibly, and took Albert from Angela with hardly a smile, plopped him back in the trolley with the now bagged shopping and started counting out a few notes before making up the remaining balance of a few pounds and pence with assorted coins.

"Would you like a car parking ticket?" asked Angela brightly as the couple and Albert prepared to leave.

"Yes please," said the woman,

"They're five pounds today," she said matter-of-factly.

"In that case I'll have to put something back," said the woman quietly, desperate to avoid the alternative of a usurious fine, as she reached into the bag and pulled out a bottle of supermarket own-brand moisturiser.

"That should cover it," she muttered as she put the small container on the side.

"I'm having none of it," said Dr Godfrey stiffly and without warning, from the other end of the conveyor belt. "Angela, put the five pounds on my bill and let the young couple have a parking ticket. Horace and Charlie turned to examine Dr Godfrey more closely as the couple thanked him profusely and went on their way. The woman looked close to tears. Dr Godfrey leant over the conveyor belt, took Angela's hand and kissed it. Angela blushed.

"And how are you today, my darling?" he asked as the customer behind him sighed loudly. Angela turned round to see where the suit was, saw that he was at the other end of the store talking to John so handed Dr Godfrey a small free-standing TILL CLOSED - WE WOULD BE HAPPY TO SERVE YOU AT ONE OF OUR OTHER TILLS sign which he rather ostentatiously placed behind his shopping that was already on the conveyor belt. The other customer sighed again, this time more loudly, then he and all the others behind him wandered off to find other cashiers. If they couldn't speak to Angela then they wanted to pay and get out of the supermarket as quickly as possible.

"I'm very well, Jonathan," she purred, "and I have a couple of scouts helping me today. They're bag packing. Fundraising."

"Excellent," said Dr Godfrey. "Fundraising in aid of what?"

"La Rochelle Hospice," said Charlie and Horace in unison, by now ready and well-versed in answering the questions that were thrown at them by a few sticky customers but now with their fingers crossed. In truth, there weren't many questions that were thrown at them; most, unlike Mr Gibbs, were happy to drop a few coins in the buckets and be on their way. Some customers recognised Horace or Charlie and would say something along the lines of, "Aren't you Karen's son? Gosh, you've grown," which would put the pair on guard as well as on their best behaviour. But that was

35

about it. However Dr Godfrey was already in the "sticky customer" category.

"'La Rochelle Hospice?'" he repeated. "I don't know that one. It's not anywhere in the United Kingdom, I'm sure."

"So how do you know all the hospices' names?" asked Charlie, keen to avoid identifying the mysterious hospice further.

"Because it's my job, young man. I'm a director of one locally. But I like your style! I would have done the same in my day. Much better than saying, 'We need a few tents' or suchlike. Here's twenty pounds. Now avert your ears while I speak to Angela."

Charlie and Horace looked the other way whilst Dr Godfrey whispered something to his favourite cashier. When she instructed them to turn back round to pack the doctor's bags she was blushing wildly. Dr Godfrey left with a, "Don't be late," and Angela handed the pair another twenty pound note. "I had to say 'Yes' to Dr Godfrey for this one," she said.

"'Yes' to what?" asked Horace. But Angela didn't reply. She just blushed even more. She bent down to pick up her keys and lock her till before going to lunch when another man appeared. He was smartly dressed in suit and tie but with an unshaven face and red bleary eyes which Horace thought was a bit strange for lunchtime. Neither did he appear to be the sort of person who would have a young baby in tow.

"Maybe he's just got up," thought Horace. "Maybe he had to work nights. But then who wears a suit at night when there's no one to see you?"

The tired-looking man walked up alongside the conveyor belt and quickly offloaded a few items from his basket directly in front of Angela.

"I'm sorry, but we're closed for lunch now," she said firmly without mentioning a name.

"Obviously not one of Angela's regulars," thought Horace.

"Please," said the man. "I'm in a bit of a hurry. I'll give the boys a good tip," he added, sounding almost desperate in an attempt to seal the deal. But Horace was rattled. He had heard that tone of voice earlier in the morning and it wasn't sound.

"Would you like a bag?" asked Horace solicitously once he noticed that the man had no visible means of transporting his goods. "They cost a little bit but they're reusable."

"Yes please," said the man, then held out his hand towards his groceries as Angela rapidly scanned the items through. "Don't touch."

Horace looked at him perplexed. No one had yet that morning asked for a bag but then refused the packing service. The man was soon occupied trying to get his debit card payment authorised because it had been declined. Horace meanwhile was staring at the man's groceries, especially his rather large Thermos flask. Horace thought it was a very attractive colour with a stainless steel top. He remembered that his mother had one somewhere that came out occasionally with a cooked lunch in it when his parents were going out for the day. "Your stew will keep warm for hours," she would say, but once she was out of the front

37

door Horace would be eating his lunch just in case he left it too long and the food went cold.

Horace was fascinated by the object. He knew they worked very well but wasn't exactly sure how. As the man was trying for a third time to get his payment authorised, Horace decided to ignore him and picked up the flask.

"What's this then?" he asked innocently.

"It's a Thermos," said Charlie as the man shiftily shifted from one leg to the other whilst he waited for his card finally to be authorised but made no physical attempt to stop Horace holding it.

"Leave it, it's fragile. I'll pack it," he said, his eyes darting between Horace and the card reader whilst Horace continued to examine it.

"You put cold stuff in it and it stays cold or hot stuff in and it stays hot. It's good for soups and things like that for hot and beer and stuff for cold," explained Charlie as the man left Angela pulling out and reinserting his card for a fourth time and tried to grab the Thermos from Horace. But by now Horace had moved slightly away from the man and had turned the Thermos upside down and was trying to read the writing that was printed on the black base.

"I know what it is Charlie, mummy has one just like it. I just wondered exactly how it works."

"Leave it, it's expensive," demanded the man.

"Does it come ready to use?" asked Horace shaking the Thermos gently. "Usually expensive things come in a box with a picture on the front. And like when you get helicopters or cars or games at Christmas and you also need batteries but no one's bought any or do you plug it in to warm it up?" Charlie looked at him, both smiling and frowning: smiling at Horace's frustration at the thought of his receiving a gift that he couldn't immediately play with and frowning at the inability of parents and other adults to think of keeping a few assorted batteries in their pockets at all times, especially at Christmas, unlike his Auntie Andra and her pockets always and forever stuffed full of dog chews.

"The thing is," Horace continued, "it's got stuff in it, listen." He shook the Thermos again, this time more vigorously. Horace placed it back down on the packing area and looked at the man who had not pulled his card out of the machine, not attempted to key in his PIN again and was instead patting his pockets in an attempt to find some non-existent cash. The man was now staring blankly ahead over Horace's shoulder. For standing a few feet away was, once more, Frank.

"You had better come with me, sir," said Frank to the customer. "And bring yer Thermos." He spoke curtly and unsmilingly. Something was up but the pair had no idea what.

It was not until Horace and Charlie went for their lunch break a few minutes later that word was relayed to them as to what had happened and that as a consequence they were fast becoming the talk of the supermarket staff. As they sat in the rest room munching on their packed lunch one of the cashiers told Horace that the store had not caught a shoplifter for two weeks and then, "You come along and catch two in almost as few hours!"

"'Two?'" asked Horace incredulously. "I know about Lady Willit obviously. Who was the second one?"

"Angela's last customer before lunch. The man with the dodgy debit card. The one with the Thermos. The reason that you could hear something in the Thermos was because it was full of malt whisky. Harry's the manager and he's just found two empty bottles on the shelf. So although he was trying to pay for the Thermos, he wasn't going to be paying for the whisky. He's denied knowing about it of course, like you pick up a Thermos without realising that there's something sloshing around inside. But there will be fingerprints on the bottles as well as a bit of surveillance film because we always keep an eye on the booze part of the store. It never ceases to amaze me that people that don't have the means to pay pick on expensive items like spirits when I would have thought that food would be a far more desirable option. Like a frozen chicken! Anyway, well done Horace!"

When Horace and Charlie went back to bag packing after lunch they had a real spring in their step. They were invincible! Word of their antics had spilled out onto the street - some parts of it at least - and they were rapidly becoming as popular as Angela. They began helping everyone with packing their bags whether they liked it or not. Angela's queue grew once more. No one wanted to use the self-service checkouts - they remained free and even the other cashiers weren't so busy. Horace would shake everything before he put it in the customer's bag, even bottles with genuine liquid in them - as well as peering at the contents. He had even started to unscrew every bottle and give it a sniff but Angela soon put a stop to that particular activity. "How do we know that what's in the bottle is what's supposed to be in there?" he asked. "They could've swapped cheap squash for brandy."

"You're a bag packer," said Angela smiling, "not a sniffer dog. Security will act on suspicions but we're not looking for suspicions, we wait for them to come to us."

"But no one would've picked up on that man's Thermos," complained Horace, "if I hadn't shaken it." Angela sighed.

"Oh Horace, when you're older I'm sure that there will be a job for you in surveillance but for now just stick to bag packing and fleecing customers for our possibly maybe not phantom hospice. Restrict the shaking to your collecting bucket, but not too vigorously; we don't want the customers to know how much we've already amassed, do we?"

"Spare a few coins for the poor scouts" was Charlie's new cry, followed by Horace adding, "or a few notes." The pair were working well together and the collecting buckets were filling up. Horace and Charlie were gaining even more confident; they had realised the importance of establishing a rapport with the shoppers even with the limited time they had with each one at their disposal. Men were tipping less often but with more; most women gave a least a few coins. Towards the middle of the afternoon a man came through wearing a large brimmed hat. Angela did not refer to him by name so the pair assumed that he was an irregular. Nevertheless, Horace asked the man if he could try his hat on. The reply wasn't what he expected.

"No, bog off kid," said the man abruptly. Horace immediately took a dislike to him. He did not like being told to "bog off," even less the man's face which showed signs of a possible violent past. As Horace stared at him whilst he was paying Horace was shocked to see what looked like a trickle of blood coming out from under his hat and down the side of his forehead.

"Charlie, can you remind me, have you done level one emergency aid badge yet?" Yes, he had. "Can you stop bleeding?" Yes, he can. In that case, Horace looked at the man and instead of asking for a donation said,

"Excuse me sir, but your face is bleeding."

"It's nothing, bog off," said the man shortly, implying that he knew about the blood and unintentionally confirming that there was something odd about it. "After all," thought Horace, "who would not want to be treated, and immediately, when they knew that they were bleeding?"

"But sir, my colleague Charlie here is almost a paramedic nearly. He can attend to cuts, burns and scalds - and fainting. You're not about to faint are you?"

"Bog off, bog off, bog off," repeated the man irritably, sounding like a psychiatric parrot. However, the pair of, by now, self-styled seasoned store detectives were going to do nothing of the sort. As the man marched past Horace Charlie picked up a broom from the vacant till next to them and placed the free end of the handle under the rim of the man's hat. He then pushed swiftly up as the man walked past John who had come over to see what the minor commotion was all about this time. The hat flicked cleanly off the man's head, span in the air and landed neatly on the ground.

"You can't pick it up, can you?" Horace suggested to the man, "'Cos you've got a couple of filet steaks on top of your head haven't you?! Fr – ank! Fr – ank!" However, with remarkably bad timing Frank was not in the vicinity and was not manning the security cameras. When he eventually arrived Horace told him what had happened and that the man had run off leaving the steaks.

"Come over here," said Frank, taking the pair away from the checkouts. "What did he look like?" he asked as he sat them both down on a small bench.

"Like this," said Charlie, getting out his 'phone. "I took a picture of him."

"You two are going to do me out of a job," Frank said with a big grin on his face.

"No we're not, we're just proving that you're needed," said Horace conciliatorily. "Now if you were thinking of throwing those steaks away, can you give them to us to take home? They'll only need a little wash."

"Of course," said Frank. "I'll go and put them in one of the fridges out the back. Now off you go and help Angela. You're doing really well and you haven't got very long left."

When Horace and Charlie went back to their positions Horace was surprised to find his mother being served. Saturday was not normally a day for supermarket shopping in the Horrise household and, so far as Horace was aware, never in this particular supermarket. Mrs Horrise had already paid and packed her own bag and was looking very surprised at what Angela had to say with her back to the pair. "The thing is, madam, although they're not here at this particular moment they will be back soon and they've been very busy helping pack bags so if you wouldn't mind making a small donation to St Rochelle Hospice?"

"'St Rochelle Hospice?' I thought that they were fundraising for a patrol tent."

"Oh no, no, no, no, no," said Angela, unsure as to how her latest customer was so well informed. "It's definitely the Hospice."

"Well, perhaps we can ask the scouts themselves what they're fundraising for," she replied as she spied Horace and Charlie advancing.

"Hello mummy," said Horace brightly. Pre-empting her question Horace continued, "We're fundraising, that's all I suggest that you need to know."

"In that case," said his mother, "you'd better keep an eye on your cashier lest she gets you into a whole load of trouble. And what's this rumour I've been hearing all over Chislehurst this lunchtime that you've been catching thieves?"

"We'll be fine Mrs Horrise," said Charlie.

"All will be revealed at home later mummy," said Horace as she marched off, "and don't go out that way 'cos I don't want Mel to see you."

"And I don't want to be seen by Mel," said Horace's mother as she rapidly turned on her heels and walked out through the other door. Angela shrugged her shoulders.

"You win some, you lose some," she said and turned to serve her next customer, but not before Horace had asked her what his mother had bought.

"A frozen chicken and some filet steak," said Angela.

"Did she put them in her bag or under her hat?" asked Charlie as straight-faced as he could manage. "OW!"

"Hello Mrs Jones. How's your eye? We have some scouts fundraising today for a very important cause..."

***

Horace and Charlie were sitting at the front of the supermarket on a small ledge by a stack of free newspapers, that no one was taking, near the supermarket entrance. They were having a short break when they were shocked to see Mel's mother in not only the supermarket but also in Angela's queue. As she was waving at Horace he stood up and walked round to say hello.

Melanie's mother pulled down her sunglasses and peered over the top of them.

"Where's my daughter?" she asked conspiratorially.

"Up the other end," said Horace. "But Angela can serve you." No chance.

"Thanks darling," she said and marched off. Horace noticed that she only had one item in her basket - a bottle of very expensive-looking Champagne.

A man came in dressed in what Horace's mother would have described as "rough clothes," and dirty ones at that, together with dirty hair and dirty fingernails. Pushing an empty trolley he walked slowly up to the pair, bent down and asked them in a low voice if they could do him a favour. "You see this," he said, pressing a shopping list into their hands. "Can ya go and get all the stuff that's on it and put it in this trolley? I've put loads of carrier bags in there as well. Put the stuff in them first. I'll give ya a good tip."

Horace and Charlie thought that they may not yet be the winners of the fundraising competition and that there was still all to play for so they readily agreed even though the last person to promise them "a good tip" came up with precisely nothing. "Once we have 'the stuff,' what do we do?" asked Horace, always keen to get any instructions clear in his mind before execution.

"Ya bring it round to the back door of the supermarket and go straight through into the car park. I'll be waiting out there in my white van. I've put the registration number on the bottom of the list so ya get the right one. Put my shopping list in one of the bags, open the van's back doors 'cos they'll be unlocked, throw the stuff in and come round to the passenger door for ya big tip."

"How about a very big tip?"

"Yep. No probs."

"That's fine," said Horace. "But what about paying?"

"It's prepaid. I've paid already. It's like 'click and collect' only it's called 'pay and pack' 'cos the customer does the packing and not the shop assistant. I go online and put my list onto my account and the supermarket works out how much it is and I pay and it's a bit cheaper. All I then have to do is pick the items and load up. Off you go."

"What a great idea!" said Horace. "I shall tell mummy about it when I get home!"

"You do that sunshine. Now off you go! Get on with it."

"Come on Charlie," said Horace. "We've got a few minutes before we have to go back to Angela. We can squeeze this job in!"

Horace took the list and started to push the trolley up and down the aisles as Charlie picked and packed all the while imagining that maybe the fundraising competition was ever so possibly starting to be in their bag. However a troubling thought had hit Horace and it wouldn't go away. Horace stopped pushing for a moment and said, "What I don't understand, Charlie, is why the man doesn't come and do his shopping normally? What's the point of ordering and paying before you come shopping 'cos it can't be that cheaper?"

"Or why doesn't he get it delivered? And why does he need so much whisky and perfume?" asked Charlie looking down the list.

"Maybe his wife is a smelly alcoholic," said Horace light-heartedly although he was looking deadly serious, for something else was troubling him. "This is going to be the biggest bag packing we've done today and yet if the man has ordered and paid online how does he get his Vitality Vouchers 'cos you can only get them from the store and if he's so concerned about cost then he's not going to miss out on them is he?"

"I don't know, and as far as I'm concerned, they're just like money," replied Charlie. "What can we do to get hold of them for ourselves?"

"All we have to do is go through Angela's till on the way out and tell her to run off the vouchers for us before we take the trolley outside. With all this food not forgetting drinks and smells it must be worth at least a few hundred tent pegs as a minimum."

"Good idea," agreed Charlie.

Horace and Charlie finished off their picking, spending much of their time in the spirits and perfume sections, before making their way gingerly towards the till where they had spent most of the day so far.

"Hi Angela," said Horace beaming.

"Come on boys," said Angela encouragingly. "I've been open again for at least twenty minutes and I'm having to do all your work as well! And what are you doing with that trolley load of booze? I can't sell you that!"

"No, it's okay," said Horace innocently. "We've been asked to do a 'pick and pack' by a nice man who's about to give us a great big tip but we don't think he's been given his Vitality Vouchers so can we have them please and can you put them in our collecting buckets?"

"Just a mo," said Angela. "You've been asked to do what?"

"Pick and pack."

"'Pick and pack!' What's that then?! There's no such thing! We do 'click and collect' though. Did you mean that?"

"No, the man said 'pick and pack.' He's prepaid online. Look," said Horace, pulling out the list of whisky, vodka, gin, brandy, eau de toilette, perfume, after shave... "We just had to pack it for him and wheel it out. He's waiting in a white van in the car park. This is his registration number so we get the right vehicle."

"It looks as though he needs a van with that lot." Angela pressed a button down by her knee. "Let's get Harry to sort this one out."

Harry appeared inside thirty seconds. He knew that Angela's was the hot till this particular day, and it wasn't over yet. Horace and Charlie explained what they had been asked to do and why they were now at Angela's till which she had just put her TILL CLOSED sign on.

"Right, this is a big one," said Harry. "The police are on their way now."

"How do you do that?" asked Horace who had yet to realise exactly what was going on. "How do you contact the police like that without 'phoning them?"

"I can't tell you that sort of thing Horace because it's security. The police will be here very shortly and within five minutes they'll have the car park entrance closed because they've heard what's happening."

"But how..?" Horace began to ask.

"Don't worry Horace. It's all under control. Just you boys go out and start loading the van so that it doesn't look suspicious. But do it slow, nice and slow. Real slow."

"Don't worry, we won't let him get away Harry. We're getting quite good at this," said Horace and they both chuckled. They knew from past experience with some of their other activities that if they wanted to go nice and slow they could and they could go so slowly that to the untrained eye it might appear that they had actually stopped. Horace and Charlie grinned at each other before wheeling the shopping trolley out into the car park. As soon as they walked through the supermarket doors and looked around a rusty old white van with the matching registration number drew up alongside them. The man wound down the window on the passenger side, leant over the seat, stuck his head partially out of the window and shouted, "Throw the bags in the back quick but be careful of me Scotch. Quick, quick, you've got thirty seconds at the most. The quicker you do it the more you get paid. I'm in a big 'urry."

"Just one thing," said Horace calmly. "I would be very upset if you were in such a big 'urry that you forgot to pay us so what I would like to suggest is, why don't you pay us first? You see it's a bit like 'pick and pack.' You pay in advance and it's a bit cheaper."

"I ain't in that much of an 'urry that I'm goin' to forget," said the man from inside the van, sounding increasingly frustrated, "but I can't pay ya until I know how quick you've bin. And I am in quite a bit of an 'urry, so 'urry up 'cos I'm now in more of an 'urry than I was a few seconds ago. Or do ya want me to come and load up and then you won't git nuffin?!"

The man started to become even more agitated so Horace said, "It's alright, Charlie's opened your back doors already and is loading up."

Charlie had pushed the trolley round to the back of the van and had indeed opened the doors but then all he had done was sit with his feet on the back bumper and bounce up and down a bit to simulate loading in progress.

"Well, you go an' 'elp 'im then. Go on. Quick! Now!"

"I can't I'm afraid," said Horace calmly.

"Why not yer repugnant rag?"

"I'm afraid that I'm suffering from a bad back and I mustn't lift anything heavy. The doctor says that I mustn't do anything that might make the problem worse. It could be irreparable if I'm not careful."

"What, at your age?"

"I'm actually quite old. Older than you probably think. Have a guess at how old I am."

"No. Stop yer natterin' an' go and do the lighter stuff can't ya?"

"I'm sorry, but we didn't pack for you very well 'cos we're very inexperienced you see. We just put the stuff in bags all together as we went round. But never mind, next time you come to the supermarket we'll know and we'll do it properly. Will you be here next week 'cos if you tell us in advance once you've placed your order we can come and pick it for you for even a small tip?" Sadly for Horace he did not get an answer but his delaying tactics had worked because at that moment two police cars appeared at the one and only entrance which was also the exit and parked across it. Six police officers jumped out and came running towards the van, truncheons and various other defence implements in their hands. The man's head disappeared back inside the van and he started to drive towards the cars with Charlie still sitting on the back, his feet on the rickety bumper and with the loose doors flapping but after a few seconds the man realised that the game was up. He stopped his van and was quickly hauled out by the officers. As he was handcuffed and escorted round the side of the vehicle he noticed that all that was in the back was a grinning Charlie and not a single bag.

"You ain't even started you little ruffian," he growled.

"I didn't want to have to put everything in the back of your van only to have to get it all out again once you were arrested," he said with disarming logic.

Harry came running out and told the pair that after all the excitement of the day they would be able to go home early. "What about the fundraising competition?" asked Horace. "We must win and if we go home early then we may lose to the others who are staying."

"Don't worry," said Harry. "Given the amount that I'm just about to authorise for the supermarket to add to your collection buckets, following your adventures, I don't expect that any of the other pairs will come close to what you've raised."

"Fantastic," said Horace. "But before we leave, can we just go and get our steaks and say 'good-bye' to Angela?"

***

The following Friday John was in an exceedingly good mood. The scouts spent the evening speculating on which pair had won the cash prize for raising the most at the supermarket the previous week.

John made the scouts wait until the end of the meeting, but after the usual reflections, prayers and badge distribution he announced, "We now come to the results of the bag packing last Saturday at the supermarket. It was, in many ways, quite an unusual few hours and no more so than because Horace and Charlie turned store detectives and have been responsible for more than one regular criminal being caught. The supermarket had been victim to a number of thefts this year but were having great problems with identifying who was or were responsible. As a result I have two "Well Done" certificates that I hardly ever give out and the supermarket has also produced a couple of certificates as well as a gift token each. So come forward and receive these please, Horace and Charlie. And whilst they are coming out I also have to tell you all that the supermarket also donated five hundred pounds to their fundraising effort. So 'well done' for that as well because the amount that you raised is enough to buy a couple of new patrol tents all by yourselves."

Horace and Charlie stepped out of their line to enthusiastic applause. "I don't understand it," Mel whispered to Emily though the clapping. "How could they have raised so much?" Emily shrugged her shoulders and continued to join in with the approbation.

Horace and Charlie returned to their places, ready to walk back up to John to receive their cash prize.

"Now as you will recall," continued John, "last week I said

that the pair that raised the most could keep the difference between what they and what the pair in second place raised. Which is 'well done' to them because the pair in third place was well behind the second, but the pair that raised the most, by a margin - a margin! - of over two thousand pounds is..." The scouts all gasped, Horace and Charlie smirked, Mel and Emily scowled. "...Mel and Emily! I don't know how you did it but you did. So step forward girls!"

"I don't believe it Charlie," whispered Horace through the clapping. "A thousand pounds each? That's a sweet shop! How could they have raised so much?"

"Probably thanks to someone very near to one of them who's already toasted success with a glass or three of Champagne," lamented Horace.

"Horace and Charlie came second and they also collected a record number of Vitality Vouchers, in fact enough to buy not one but two new four-man tents quite apart from the patrol tent that we're after. So 'well done' to them again and I've decided to award you both a cash prize also because you've done so well. So scouts, collectively you've all earned your evening at Swingers with refreshments on Mel and Emily and in the meantime I'm going to let the winners and runners-up also have, within reason, anything of your choice that the scout section can all benefit from. What's it to be?"

"I would like to have one investiture please, Skip, Everyone can benefit from that!" said Horace without a second's hesitation and the scouts all laughed.

"I think that it would have to be pizzas all round please Skip, and not one of Archie's recipes please," said Mel.

"A fantastic idea Mel. I'll order twenty or so margheritas for next week."

"And a raspberry and Marmite for Edward," said Charlie.

"I would like you to make sure, Skip, that every scout has a go on the Grunt course and no one's allowed to dip out," said Emily. Horace scowled.

***

A couple of weeks later on a Saturday morning Horace and Charlie popped into the supermarket looking to find Angela to thank her once more for her help in indirectly winning them both a not insubstantial amount of cash. They walked in the main door and within seconds found themselves being escorted out the back and into the car park by Frank. "We've only come to see Angela," said a bemused Horace.

"Angela doesn't work here anymore," said Frank stiffly. "She's been let go. Now buzz off and don't come back unless you're with a parent."

"When was she 'let go?'" asked Horace.

"Yesterday," said Frank.

"Why?" asked Horace curiously.

"You'll find out soon enough," said Frank curtly.

"Why are you being so horrible to us?" asked Charlie with a puzzled frown.

"You'll find out soon enough," Frank repeated.

And they did.

The adventure golf the following Saturday was a great success as usual. Emily was the only one to manage a (another) hole in one on the seventeenth of Grunt. All the scouts were in attendance bar two. Mel and Emily bought everyone a pizza, an ice cream and a drink but Horace and Charlie missed it. They were in the scout hut washing the floor, tidying all the kit and cleaning to a shine every single piece of cooking equipment plus all the pots, pans and utensils, and washing and drying the crockery and cutlery. It took them a whole weekend.

***

If you enjoyed "Horace Horrise catches a Shoplifter" please check out my website www.inyougo.webeden.co.uk or www.amazon.co.uk for details of my other Horace Horrise books.

Please also leave a Goodreads (www.goodreads.com) or Amazon review. I would be very grateful. On Amazon - find "Horace Horrise catches a Shoplifter" at www.amazon.co.uk and scroll down to and click on "Write a customer review" then "Submit".

Hampton Hall
Chislehurst
BR7 6PE

Dear Sir / Madam

You will be aware that 3rd Chislehurst Scouts were recently engaged in a fundraising activity in your supermarket.

In a moment of temporary lucidity in an otherwise degrading and contrary memory, I recall that I made a donation of one hundred pounds at your employee Angela's till. This wasn't the first time that I have been asked to contribute. In fact, whenever I see Angela she is collecting for one charity or other. Usually I have never heard of the charities that she mentions but this time was different.

St Rochelle Hospice in Algeria is where my late wife spent her final days. I know of no other by that name. One of the scouts mentioned that his grandmother had been recently cared for there also which was an impossibility given that the hospice closed MANY years ago.

Like someone from the "posh part of town" in Oliver Twist I feel that I have been hoodwinked by a modern-day female Fagin and a couple of her boys taking advantage of my current precarious medical condition and so I am writing to advise you that, as long as I can remember not to, I will never ever be setting foot in your store again.

I remain,
Yours faithfully
Mr Gibbs

ALSO AVAILABLE BY JOHN HEMMING-CLARK

In You Go!
A Year or Two in the Life of a Scout Leader
Paperback: £9.99 ISBN: 9781897864265
"...this is one of the funniest books I have ever read." Amazon review

Sleeping Bags & Tortures. The Private Diaries of an Adventurous Scout & his Scout Leader
Paperback £9.99 ISBN 9781897864326
Hardback £16.99 ISBN 9781897864302
A brilliant book, I couldn't put it down. By presenting the story through the eyes of both a Scout and their Leader you get a great insight into the crazy adventures of the 3rd Chislehurst Scout Troop..."
Amazon review

1000 Fantastic Scout Games
Paperback £9.99 ISBN 9781897864296
"Great book, fantastic to have so many games to hand ..."
"A lot of new ideas covering indoor and outdoor games with easy to follow instructions. I highly recommend this to any Scout or play groups and is suitable for all sections and ages." Amazon reviews

250 No Equipment Games
Paperback: £6.99 ISBN 9781897864388
"Perfect for the times when you go to get a ball and the cubs have taken them all to camp, or you haven't planned a game and it needs a new one. Some in, some out, some noisy, some quiet, something for everyone." Amazon review

Letters Home from Scout and Guide Camp
Paperback £1.99 ISBN 9781897864364
"I took this book to our cub camp and the children as well as the adults really enjoyed it. Very funny - a lot of fun. This book is "very enjoyable" by all ages. It made an evening of excellent entertainment."
Amazon review

Available online from www.inyougo.webeden.co.uk or (inc. download) www.amazon.co.uk.   Cards: Tel: 020 8468 7945.
Cheques: ("Searchline Publishing") Searchline House, 1A Holbrook Lane, Chislehurst, BR7 6PE